1935 ...
read a goo...
either a lot of m... ...brary card.
Cheap paperbacks ... ...e available, but their
poor production generally mirrored the quality
between the covers. One weekend that year,
Allen Lane, Managing Director of The Bodley Head,
having spent the weekend visiting Agatha Christie,
found himself on a platform at Exeter station trying to
find something to read for his journey back to London.
He was appalled by the quality of the material he had to
choose from. Everything that Allen Lane achieved from that
day until his death in 1970 was based on a passionate belief
in the existence of 'a vast reading public for *intelligent*
books at a low price'. The result of his momentous vision
was the birth not only of Penguin, but of the 'paperback
revolution'. Quality writing became available for the price of
a packet of cigarettes, literature became a mass medium
for the first time, a nation of book-borrowers became a
nation of book-buyers – and the very concept of book
publishing was changed for ever. Those founding
principles – of quality and value, with an overarching
belief in the fundamental importance of reading –
have guided everything the company has
done since 1935. Sir Allen Lane's
pioneering spirit is still very much alive
at Penguin in 2005. Here's to
the next 70 years!

MORE THAN A BUSINESS

'We decided it was time to end the almost customary half-hearted manner in which cheap editions were produced – as though the only people who could possibly want cheap editions must belong to a lower order of intelligence. We, however, believed in the existence in this country of a vast reading public for intelligent books at a low price, and staked everything on it'
Sir Allen Lane, 1902–1970

'The Penguin Books are splendid value for sixpence, so splendid that if other publishers had any sense they would combine against them and suppress them'
George Orwell

'More than a business ... a national cultural asset'
Guardian

'When you look at the whole Penguin achievement you know that it constitutes, in action, one of the more democratic successes of our recent social history'
Richard Hoggart

Otherwise Pandemonium

NICK HORNBY

PENGUIN BOOKS

PENGUIN BOOKS

Published by the Penguin Group
Penguin Books Ltd, 80 Strand, London WC2R ORL, England
Penguin Group (USA) Inc., 375 Hudson Street, New York, New York 10014, USA
Penguin Group (Canada), 10 Alcorn Avenue, Toronto, Ontario, Canada M4V 3B2
(a division of Pearson Penguin Canada Inc.)
Penguin Ireland, 25 St Stephen's Green, Dublin 2, Ireland
(a division of Penguin Books Ltd)
Penguin Group (Australia), 250 Camberwell Road, Camberwell, Victoria 3124,
Australia (a division of Pearson Australia Group Pty Ltd)
Penguin Books India Pvt Ltd, 11 Community Centre,
Panchsheel Park, New Delhi – 110 017, India
Penguin Group (NZ), cnr Airborne and Rosedale Roads, Albany,
Auckland 1310, New Zealand (a division of Pearson New Zealand Ltd)
Penguin Books (South Africa) (Pty) Ltd, 24 Sturdee Avenue,
Rosebank 2196, South Africa

Penguin Books Ltd, Registered Offices: 80 Strand, London WC2R ORL, England

www.penguin.com

'Otherwise Pandemonium' first published in
McSweeney's Mammoth Treasury of Thrilling Tales
in the USA 2002
Published in Penguin Books 2004
This selection published as a Pocket Penguin 2005

1

Copyright © Nick Hornby, 2005
All rights reserved

Set in 11/13pt Monotype Dante
Typeset by Palimpsest Book Production Limited
Polmont, Stirlingshire
Printed in England by Clays Ltd, St Ives plc

Contents

Otherwise Pandemonium

Mom always sings this crappy old song when I'm in a bad mood. She does it to make me laugh, but I never do laugh, because I'm in a bad mood. (Sometimes I sort of smile later, when I'm in a better mood, and I think about her singing and dancing and making the dorky black-and-white movie face – eyes wide, all her teeth showing – she always makes when she sings the song. But I never tell her she makes me smile. It would only encourage her to sing more often.) This song is called 'Ac-cent-chu-ate the Positive', and I have to listen to it whenever she tells me we're going to Dayton to see Grandma, or when she won't give me the money for something I need, like CDs or even clothes, for Christ's sake. Anyway, today I'm going to do what the song says. I'm going to accentuate the positive, and eliminate the negative. Otherwise, according to the song and to my mom, pandemonium is liable to walk upon the scene.

OK. Well, here is the accentuated positive: I got to have sex. That's the upside of it. I know that's probably a strange way of looking at things, considering the circumstances, but it's definitely the major event of the week so far. It won't be the major event of the year, I know that – Jesus, do I know that – but it's still a head-line news item: I just turned fifteen, and I'm no longer a virgin. How cool is that? The target I'd set for myself was sixteen, which means I'm a whole year ahead of schedule. Nearly two years, in fact, because I'll still be sixteen in twenty-two months' time. So let's say this is the story of how I ended up getting laid – a story with a beginning, and a weird middle, and a happy ending. Otherwise I'd have to tell you a Stephen King-type story, with a beginning and a weird middle and a really fucking scary ending, and I don't want to do that. It wouldn't help me right now.

So. You probably think you need to know who I am, and what kind of car my brother drives, and all that Holden Caulfield kind of crap, but you really don't, and not just because I haven't got a brother, or even a cute little sister. It's not one of those stories. Insights into my personality and all that stuff aren't going to help you or me one bit, because this shit is real. I don't want you to get to the end of this and start thinking about whether I'd have acted different if my parents had stayed together, or whether I'm a typical product of our times, or what I tell you about being fifteen, or any of those other questions we have to discuss when we read a story in school. It's not the point. All you need to know is where I got the video recorder from, and maybe, I suppose, why I got it, so I'll tell you.

I found it a couple blocks from my house, in this store that sells used electronic stuff. It cost fifty bucks, which seemed pretty good to me, although now it doesn't seem like such a great bargain, but that's another story. Or

rather, it's this story, but a different part of it. And I
bought it because . . . OK, so maybe I will have to give
you a little background, but I won't make it into a big
drama. I'll just give you the facts. My mom and I moved
from L.A. to Berkeley about three months ago. We
moved because Mom finally walked out on my asshole
of a father, who writes movies for a living – although
as none of them ever got made, it would be more accu-
rate to say that he writes scripts for a living. Mom is an
art teacher, and she paints her own stuff, too, and she
says there are millions of people in Berkeley with an
artistic bend or whatever, so she thought we'd feel right
at home here. (I like it that she says 'we'. I haven't got
an artistic bone in my whole body, and she knows that,
but for some reason she thinks I take after her. It was
pretty much always me and her against him, so that
became me and her against L.A., and because I was
against L.A., that somehow made me able to paint. I
don't mind. Painting's pretty cool, some of it.)

Berkeley's nice, I guess, but I didn't have any friends
here, so Mom made me join this dumb jazz orchestra
thing. I'd just started to take trumpet lessons in L.A.,
and I didn't suck too bad; a couple months after we
moved, she saw an ad in a local bookstore for something called the Little Berkeley Big Band, which is like
for people under the age of seventeen, and she signed
me up. She had to sing the Ac-cent-chu-ate song a lot
in the car the first evening I went to a rehearsal, because
I'd be the first to admit that I wasn't feeling very positive. But it was OK, not that I'd ever admit that to her.

You can make a pretty fucking great noise when you're part of a horn section. I can't say I'm going to make any friends, though. The kind of people who want to play in the Little Berkeley Big Band . . . well, let's just say that they're not my kind of people. Apart from Martha, but I'll tell you about her later. (And now you'll probably have guessed some of the ending, but I don't care, because you only know her name, and not how we ended up having sex. How we ended up having sex is the interesting part.) All you need to know about Martha: a) She's hot; b) but hot in a not-slutty way. In other words, if you saw her, you would never guess in a million years that I'd persuade her to sleep with me. (Hopefully that has made you very curious – 'Man, how the fuck did he get to sleep with her?' – which means you'll be more interested in the happy ending, rather than the weird middle, which means I don't have to take the Stephen King route.)

But my argument for the video recorder was this: not only was I not making friends at the band rehearsals, but the rehearsals were actually *stopping* me from making friends. Here's how that works: I go to rehearsals. We don't have a VCR. (We left ours in L.A. with Dad, and for some insane reason Mom didn't want to buy a replacement right away, I guess because we were supposed to read books and paint and play trumpets every night, like we were living in the Little House on the Prairie or something.) I can't tape the NBA playoffs. I can't talk about the games next day. Everyone thinks I'm a dweeb. Obvious, right? Not to her. I had to threaten to go back and live with Dad before she gave in, and even then she more or less told me I had to find the cheapest, crappiest machine in the Bay Area.

Anyway, it's pretty great, this place. It sells old TVs – like really old, Back-to-the-Future old – and guitars, and amps, and stereos and radios. And VCRs. I just asked the old hippy guy who runs the place for the cheapest one he had that actually worked, and he pointed me over to this pile right in the corner of the store.

'That one on the top works,' he said. 'Or at least, it was working a few days ago. Used to be mine.'

'So why aren't you using it anymore?' I asked him. I was trying to be sharp, but that doesn't often work for me. Give me an hour or two and I'm sharp as a box cutter, but sometimes in the moment, things don't work out as good as I'd want.

'I got a better one,' he said. I couldn't really argue with that. He could probably have made one that was better. Shit, I could probably have made one that was better.

'But it records?'

He just looked at me.

'Records and plays?'

'No, kid. It does everything else, just doesn't record or play.'

'So if it doesn't record or play, what's the point . . .' Then I realized he was being sarcastic, so of course I felt pretty dumb.

'And you never had any trouble with it?'

'Depends what you mean by trouble.'

5

'Like . . . with recording? Or playing?' I couldn't think of another way of putting it.

'No.'

'So what sort of trouble did you have?'

'If this conversation lasts any longer, I'll have to put the price up. Otherwise it's not worth my time.'

'Does it come with a remote?'

'I can find you one.'

So I just dug in my pocket for the fifty bucks, handed it to him, and went and got the thing off the top of the pile. He found a remote and put it in my jacket pocket. And then, as I was walking out, he said this weird thing.

'Just . . . forget it.'

'What?'

'I did.'

'What?'

This guy was old-school Berkeley, if you know what I mean. Grey beard, grey pony-tail, dirty old vest.

'Cos it can't know anything, right? It's just a fucking VCR. What can it know? Nothing.'

'No, man,' I said. Because I thought I had a handle on him then, you know? He was nuts, plain and simple. Weed had destroyed his mind. 'No, it can't know anything. Like you say, what could it know?'

He smiled then, like he was really relieved, and it was only when he smiled that I could tell how sad he looked before.

'I really needed to hear that,' he said.

'Happy to oblige.'

'I'm forty-nine years old, and I got a lot to do. I got a novel to write.'

'You'd better hurry.'

'Really?' He looked worried again. I didn't know what the fuck I'd said.

'Well. You know. Hurry in your own time.' Because I didn't care when he wrote his stupid novel. Why should I?

'Right. Right. Hey, thanks.'

'No problem.'

And that was it. I thought about what he'd said for maybe another minute and a half, and then forgot about him. For a while, anyway.

So I was all set. I had a band rehearsal that night, so I wired the VCR up to the TV in my room, and then I did a little test on it. I recorded some news show for a couple minutes, and then I played it back – A-okay. I checked out the remote – fine. I even put my tape of *The Matrix* in the machine, to see what kind of picture quality I was getting. (The kind of picture quality you get on a fifty-buck VCR was what I was getting.) Then I worked out the timer, and set it for the last part of that night's Lakers game. Everything was cool. Or rather, everything would have been cool, if my mom hadn't decided to interfere, although as it turned out, it was a good sort of interference.

What happened was, I got a lift home from Martha's dad. With Martha in the car. I mean, of course Martha was in the car, because that was why her dad had turned up at the community center, but, you know. Martha was in the car. Which meant . . . well, not too much, if you really want to analyse it that closely. I didn't talk a whole lot. Like I said, give me a few hours to think about it and I'm William fucking Shakespeare; I'm just not so good in real time. I guess it's my dad's genes coming through. He can write OK dialogue if he has enough time to think about it – like a year. But ask him the simplest question, like 'What's going on with you and Mom?' and he's, you know, 'Duh, yeah, well, blah.' Thanks, Dad. That's made things real clear.

Anyway, we got in the car, and . . . Oh – first of all, I should tell you that it's turning into a regular thing, which is how come I wasn't too disgusted by my performance that night. And maybe I should confess that I nearly blew it, too. This is where Mom's good/bad interference comes in. What happened was, she dropped into this little gallery in the neighborhood, to see if they'd be interested in exhibiting her stuff, and she got talking to the owner, who turns out to be Martha's dad. And somehow they got on to the subject of the Little Berkeley Big Band, and like two seconds later they've divided up the rides. I'll be honest here: I completely freaked out when she told me. No amount of singing her song would have calmed me down. She explained that she met this guy who lives real near and his daughter was in the band and so he was going to drop us off and pick us up this week and it was her turn next week and . . .

'Stop right there.'

'What?'

'Do you realize what a bunch of pathetic losers they are in that band? You really expect me to sit in a car with one of them every week?'

'I'm not asking you to date her. I'm asking you to sit in a car with her for ten minutes once a week.'

'No way.'

'Too late.'

'Fine. I'm quitting the band. As from this second.'

'You don't think that's an overreaction?'

'No. Goodbye.'

And I went up to my bedroom. I meant it. I was going to quit. I didn't care. Even if I was giving up a future career as a superstar jazz trumpeter, it was worth it if it meant not sitting in a car with Eloise and her bad breath. Or Zoe and her quote unquote gland problem (in other words her intense fatness problem.) Anyway, Mom came up five minutes later and said that she'd called the guy and canceled the ride, told him I had a doctor's appointment first so I wouldn't be leaving from home.

'A doctor's appointment? Great, so now everyone thinks I've got some gross disease. Thanks a lot.'

'Jesus.' She shook her head.

'And anyway, how am I going to get out of coming back with them?' I will admit, I was being pretty difficult.

She shook her head again. If I hadn't been so mad, I might have felt sorry for her. 'I'll think of something.'

'Like what?'

'I don't know. Just get in the car. We'll be late.'

'No. Now it's too embarrassing. I'm still quitting.'

'Paul will be disappointed. I got the impression that he had high hopes for you and Martha. He thought you sounded like . . .'

'Whoa. Martha?'

'Do you know her?'

'Maybe.'

'Do you like her?'

I tried to be cool about it. 'She's OK. I'll just go and find my trumpet.'

Respect where it's due to Mom: she didn't say anything. Didn't even smile in a way that would have made me freak out all over again. Just waited for me downstairs. She was still in the wrong, though. OK, it turned out well, but there was like a 99.9% chance (or rather, because there are maybe fifteen girls in the band, a ninety-four-point-something percent chance) that it could have been a total disaster. She didn't know it was Martha, or even who Martha is, so she was just plain lucky.

Before we get back to me in the car with Martha, which sounds way more exciting than it actually was, there's one more bit of the story that's important, but I'm not too sure where to put it. It should either go here – which was roughly where it happened – or later, when I get back from rehearsal, which is where I actually discovered it, and where it has a bit more dramatic effect. But the thing is, if I put it later, you might not believe it. You might think it's just like a story trick, or something I just made up on the spur of the moment to explain something, and it would really piss me off if you thought that. And anyway, I don't need any dramatic effects, man. This story I need to calm down, not pump up. So I'll tell you here: I messed up the VCR recording of the Lakers game. I was so mad that I watched five minutes of *The Matrix*, which meant removing the blank tape. I remembered to take out the *Matrix* tape, but I forgot to put another one back in. (I forgot because once Mom mentioned Martha, I was in kind of a hurry.) But I didn't know I'd messed up then. See what I mean? If I'd left that part until later, it might have had a little kick to it – 'Oh, no, he didn't tape the game. So how come . . .' But if that little kick means you believe me any less, it's not worth it.

Anyway, again. We got in the car after the rehearsal, me, Martha and her dad, and . . . You know what? None of this part matters. Shit, maybe I should have left the tape thing until later, because now I've brought it up, I kind of want to get back to it. I can't just keep it back for suspense purposes. And if you think about it, that's how you know most stories aren't true. I mean, I read a lot of horror writers, and those guys are always delaying the action to build it up a little. As in, I don't know, 'She ran down the path and slammed the front door with a sigh of relief. Little did she know that the Vampire Zombie was in her bathroom.

'MEANWHILE, two thousand miles away, Frank Miller of the NYPD was frowning. There was something about this case that was troubling him . . .'

See, if that shit with the Vampire Zombie was real – REAL AND HAPPENING TO YOU – you wouldn't care whether Frank Miller was frowning or not. You've got a zombie in your apartment with a fucking chainsaw or a blowtorch or something, so what does it matter what a cop does with his eyebrows on the other side of the country? Therefore, if you'll permit me to point something out that may ruin your reading pleasure forever, you know that the story has been made up.

But you know this story, the one I'm telling you, hasn't been made up. You know it a) because I told you that thing about the tape straight away, when it happened, rather than trying to get a little zinger going later, and b) because I'm not going to go into who said what to who on a car ride, just to bump up the page numbers, or to make you forget about the tape thing. You just need to hear this much: Martha and I didn't say an awful lot, but we did some smiling and whatever, so at the end of the ride we maybe both knew we liked each other. And then I got out of the car, said 'Hi' to Mom, and went upstairs to watch the game.

Well, you know now that there wasn't a tape in the machine, but I didn't. I sat down on the bed and turned on the TV. Letterman was just starting. He was doing one of those dumb list things that everyone pretends is funny but which really no one understands. I pressed the rewind on the remote: nothing. Not surprising, right? And then I pressed the fast-forward button, I guess because I thought the timer recording hadn't worked, and I wanted to check that there was a tape in there.

This is what happened: I started fast-forwarding through Letterman. I was pretty confused. How could I do that? The show wasn't even finished, so how could I have taped it? I pressed the eject, and finally I found out what you've known for a while: that there was no cassette in there. With no cassette, I can't be fast-forwarding. But my TV doesn't seem to know that, because meanwhile, Letterman's waving his hands in the air really really fast, and then we're racing through the ads, and then it's the closing credits, and then it's *The Late Late Show*, and then more ads . . . And that's when I realize what's going on: I'm fast-forwarding through network fucking television.

I mean, obviously I checked this theory out. I checked it out by keeping my finger on the remote until I got to the next morning's breakfast news, which took maybe an hour. But I got there in the end: they showed the next day's weather, and the best plays from what they said was last night's Lakers game – even though it wasn't last night to me – and, a little later, a big pile-up on the freeway near Candlestick Park that had happened in the early morning fog. I could have stopped it, if I'd known any of the drivers. I got bored after a while, and put the remote down; but it took me a long time to get to sleep.

I woke up late, and I had to rush the next morning, so I didn't get to move any further through the day's TV schedule. On my way to school, I tried to think about it all – what I could do with it, whether I'd show it to anyone, whatever. Like I said, I'm not as quick as I'd like to be. Mentally speaking, I'm not Maurice Greene. I'm more like one of those Kenyan long-distance runners. I get there in the end, but it takes like two hours and an awful lot of sweat. And to tell you the absolute truth, when I went to school that morning, I didn't see it was such a big deal. I was, like, I saw this morning's weather forecast last night; well, so what? Everyone knew what the weather was now. Same with the pile-up. And I'd seen a few of the best plays from the Lakers game, but everyone who didn't rehearse in a stupid jazz band had seen the whole game anyway. Like, I was supposed to boast to people that I'd seen stuff they saw before I did?

Imaginary conversation:

'I saw the best plays from the Lakers game.'

'So did we. We watched the game.'

'Yeah, but I saw them on the breakfast news show.'

'So did we.'

'Yeah, but I saw them on the breakfast news show last night.'

'You're a jerk. You need to have your ass kicked.'

What's fun about that? Watching breakfast news seven hours early didn't seem like such a big deal to me.

It took me a while longer than it should have done to get the whole picture: If I just kept fast-forwarding, I could see all kinds of stuff. The rest of the playoffs. The next episodes of *Buffy*, or *Friends*. The next season of *Buffy* or *Friends*. Next month's weather, whatever that's worth. Some news stuff, like, maybe, a psycho with a gun coming into our school one day next year, so I could warn the people I liked. (In other words not Brian O'Hagan. Or Mrs Fleming.) It took me longer than it should have, but I began to see that fast-forwarding through network TV could be awesome.

And for the next two days, that's all I did: I sat in my bedroom with the remote, watching the TV of the future. I watched the Lakers destroy the Pacers in the NBA finals. I watched the A's get smashed by the Yankees. I watched The One Where Phoebe and Joey Get

Married. I fast-forwarded until I got blisters. I watched TV until even my dreams got played out on a 14" screen. I was in my bedroom so often that Mom thought I had just discovered jerking off, and wanted me to call my father and talk. (Like, hello, Mom? I'm fifteen?) I could rewind, too; I could watch reruns of the TV of the future if I wanted.

And none of it was any use to me. Who wants to know stuff before it happens? People might think they do, but believe me, they don't, because if you know stuff before it happens, there's nothing to talk about. A lot of school conversation is about TV and sports; and what people like to talk about is what just happened (which I now can't remember, because it was three games back, or the episode before last) or what might happen. And when people talk about what might happen, they like to argue, or make dumb jokes; they don't want someone coming in and squashing it all flat. It's all, 'No, man, Shaq's not looking so young any more, I think the Pacers can take them.' 'No way! The Pacers have no defense. Shaq's going to destroy them.' Now, what do you say if you know the score? You tell them? Of course not. It sounds too weird, and there's nothing to bounce off anyway. So all I ever did was agree with the guy whose prediction was closest to the truth, to what I knew, and it was like I hadn't seen anything, because the knowledge I had was no fucking good to anyone. One thing I learned: School life is all about anticipation. We're fifteen, and nothing's happened to us yet, so we spend an awful lot of time imagining what things will be like. No one's interested in some jerk who says he knows. That's not what it's about.

But of course I kept going with the remote. I couldn't stop myself. I'd come back from school and watch, I'd wake up in the morning and watch, I'd come back from rehearsals and watch. I was a month, maybe five weeks, into the future – time enough to know that Frazier gets engaged to some writer, that there's a dumb new sitcom starting soon about a rock star who accidentally becomes three inches tall, and that half the Midwest gets flooded in a freak storm.

And then . . . Well, OK, maybe I should say that I had noticed something: The news programs were becoming really fucking long. It took a whole lot of fast-forwarding to get through them. And then one night I came back from school and picked up the remote, and all I could find was news. As far as I could tell, in about six weeks' time, all of network TV – every channel – is just like one long fucking news show. No *Buffy*, no sports, no nothing; just guys in suits with maps, and people in weird countries you've never heard of talking into those crappy video things which make them go all jerky and fuzzy. It was like that for a couple days after 9/11, if you remember that long ago, but sooner or later everything went back to normal; I was trying to find that part, but I couldn't get there.

Now and again I stopped to watch the people talking, but I didn't really understand it; there was stuff about India and Pakistan, and Russia, and China, and Iraq and Iran, and Israel and Palestine. There were maps, and pictures of people packing up all their shit in all these places and getting the hell out. The usual stuff, but worse, I guess.

And then, a few days' TV-time later, I found the President. I watched some of that – it was on every channel at the same time. She was sitting in the Oval Office, talking to the American people, with this really intense expression on her face. She was so serious it was scary. And she was telling us that these were the darkest days in our history, and that we were all to face them with courage and determination. She said that freedom came at a price, but that price had to be worth paying, otherwise we had no identity or value as a nation. And then she asked God to bless us all. Straight after the show they cut to live pictures of more people getting the hell out of their homes, carrying bundles of their possessions under one arm and small children under another. These people were walking down the steps of a subway station, trying to get underground. The pictures weren't fuzzy or jerky, though. These people lived in New York City.

I didn't want to watch it anymore, so I picked up the remote; never in my life have I wanted to see the opening credits of *Sabrina* so bad. But after a couple of hours of news stuff there was nothing. The TV just stops. Network TV cancelled. I've spent most of my time since then trying to see if I can get beyond the static, but I'm not there yet.

Now, all this time, I haven't spoken to anyone about any of this shit. Not to Mom, not to anyone at school, not to Martha. That's one thing they get right in stories, even though I didn't use to think so: You don't want to talk about spooky stuff. In the stories, there's always some reason for it, like, I don't know, the words don't come out when they try to speak, or the magic thing only works for the guy who's telling the story, something like that, but the real reason is, it just sounds dumb. When it finally clicked that I could watch NBA games before they happened, then obviously I thought I was going to ask a bunch of guys to come over to watch. But how do you say it? How do you say, I've got a video recorder that lets me fast-forward through the whole of TV? You don't, is the answer, unless you're a complete jerk. Can you imagine? The only quicker way to get a pounding would be to wear a STA-COOL T-shirt to school. (I just thought of something: If you're reading this, you might not know about STA-COOL. Because if you're reading this, it's way off in the future, after the static, and you might have forgotten about STA-COOL, where you are. Maybe it's a better world where people only listen to good music, not stupid pussy boy-band shit, because the world understands that life is too short for boy bands. Well, good. I'm glad. We did not die in vain.) And I was going to tell Mom, but not yet, and then when I got to the static . . . People should be allowed to enjoy their lives, is my view. Sometimes when she gives me a hard time about my clothes or playing my music loud, I want to say something. Like, 'Don't stress out, Mom, because in a month or so someone's going to drop the big one.' But most of the time I just want her to enjoy her painting, and living in Berkeley. She's happy here.

When I remembered the guy I bought the machine from, though, I wanted to speak to him. He'd seen the static too; that's what that conversation in his shop had been all about, except I didn't know it. He realized why I'd come as soon as I walked in. I didn't even say anything. He just saw it in my face.

'Oh, man,' he said after a little while. 'Oh, man. I never even started my novel.' Which I couldn't believe. I mean, Jesus. What else did this guy need to help him understand that time is running out? He'd seen the end of the fucking world on live TV, and he still hadn't gotten off his stoned ass. Although maybe he'd figured he wasn't going to find a publisher in time. And he certainly wasn't going to get too many readers.

'Maybe we're both crazy,' I said. 'Maybe we're getting it all wrong.'

'You think network TV would stop for any other reason? Like, to encourage us to get more exercise or something?'

'Maybe the thing just stopped working.'

'Yeah, and all those people were going into the subway with their kids because they couldn't find any childcare. No, we're fucked, man. I never voted for that bitch, and now she's killed me. Shit.'

At least you've had a life, I wanted to say. I haven't done anything yet. And that was when I decided to ask Martha out.

*

(OK. That was the weird middle. Now I'm going to give you the happy ending: the story of how I got to sleep with the hottest girl in the Little Berkeley Big Band, even though I'm only fifteen, and even though she doesn't look like the sort of girl who gives it up for anybody.)

One thing about knowing the world is going to end: It makes you a lot less nervous about the whole dating thing. So that's a plus. And she made it easy, anyway. We were talking in her dad's car about movies we'd seen, and movies we wanted to see, and it turned out we both wanted to see this Vin Diesel movie about a guy who can turn himself into like a bacteria any time he feels like it and hang out in people and kill them if necessary. (Although to tell you the truth, I used to want to see it more than I do now. There are a lot of things I used to want to do more than I do now. Like, I don't know, buying stuff. It sounds kind of dumb, I guess, but if you see a cool T-shirt, you're thinking about the future, aren't you? You're thinking, hey, I could wear that to Sarah Steiner's party. There are so many things connected to the future – school, eating vegetables, cleaning your teeth . . . In my position, it'd be pretty easy to let things slide.) So it seemed like the logical next step to say, hey, why don't we go together?

The movie was OK. And afterwards we went to get a pizza, and we talked about what it would be like to be a bacteria, and about the band, and about her school and my school. And then she told me that one of the reasons she liked me was that I seemed sad.

'Really?'

'Yeah. Does that sound dumb?'

'No.' Because a) nothing she says sounds dumb; b) even if it did, it would be dumb to tell her; c) I'm sad. With good reason. So I'm not surprised I look it.

'Most guys our age don't look sad. They're always laughing about nothing.'

I laughed – a little – because what she said was so true, and I hadn't even noticed it before.

'So are you really sad? Or is that just the way your face is?'

'I guess . . . I don't know. I guess I'm sad sometimes.'

'Me too.'

'Yeah? Why?'

'You first.'

Oh, man. I've seen enough movies and soaps to know that the sad guy is supposed to be the quiet, sensitive, poetic one, and I'm not sure that's me. I wasn't sad before I knew there was going to be a terrible catastrophe and we're all in trouble; suddenly, I went from like NBA fan to tortured genius-style dude. I think she's got the wrong impression. If PJ Rogers, who's this really really stupid trombonist kid in the orchestra, the kind of jerk whose wittiest joke is a loud fart, had seen what I'd seen, he'd be a tortured genius too.

'There's some stuff I'm worried about. That's all. It's not like I'm this really deep thinker.'

'Lots of kids don't worry even when there's something to worry about. They're too insensitive.'

'How about you?' I wanted to change the subject. I was getting way too much credit.

'I don't know why I'm sad half the time. I just am.'

I wanted to say to her, now, see, that's the real deal. That's being sensitive and screwed up . . . the classic Breakfast Club stuff. I'm an amateur compared to you. But I didn't. I just nodded, like I knew what she was talking about.

'Do you want to tell me about the things you're worried about? Would it help?'

'It'd help me. I think it would fuck you up.'

'I can take it.'

'I'm not sure.'

'Try me.'

And I was so sick of being on my own that I took her up on the offer. It's probably the most selfish thing I've ever done in my whole life.

I asked her over to my house for lunch, after a Saturday morning rehearsal. Mom took us back and fixed us sandwiches, and when we'd eaten we went up to my room to listen to music – or that's what she thought we were going to do. When we got upstairs, though, I explained everything, right from the beginning. I'd prepared this; I'd rewound to the point where the news started taking over the networks, and I'd found a section where they were talking about what happened when, and all the dates they mentioned were in the future. That was my evidence, and Martha believed it. It took a couple more hours to get back to the New York City subway scenes, but she wanted to see them, so we just sat there waiting. And then she watched, and then she started to cry.

*

Listen: There's something that's bothering me. Before, when I said that I asked Martha out on a date because I haven't done anything in my life yet . . . I'm not so much of an asshole that this was the first thing I thought of. It wasn't. It was one of the first, sure, but, you know – six weeks! There are lots of other things I wanted to achieve in my life, but I'm not going to get them done in six weeks. I'm not going to go to film school, and I'm not going to have a kid, and I'm not going to drive across the U.S.; at least sex is something achievable. And it's not like I was just looking for the first available piece of ass, either. I really like Martha a lot. In fact, if . . . But let's not go there. This is the happy ending, right?

Anyway. The next part came naturally. She stopped crying, and we talked, and we tried to understand what had happened. Martha knows more about that shit than I do; she said things were already pretty bad, now, in the present, but because things are happening in other countries a long ways away, I hadn't noticed. I've been watching the basketball, not the news. And then we had this real sad conversation about the stuff I'd already been thinking – about what we'd miss, and what we'd never do . . .

The truth is, she suggested it, not me. I swear. I mean, I wasn't going to say no, but it was her idea. She said that she wanted us to get good at it, which meant starting like straightaway. (She said this before, by the way. She didn't say it in response to anything, if that's what you're thinking.) So I made sure Mom was out, and then we kissed, and then we got undressed and made love in my bed. We didn't use anything. Neither of us can have any sexual disease, and if she gets pregnant, well, that's fine by us. We'd love to have a kid, for obvious reasons.

Well, that's it. That brings you up to date, whoever you are. Martha and I see each other all the time, and this weekend we're going to go away together; I'm going to tell Mom that I want to see Dad, and she's going to give her parents some other excuse, and we'll take off somewhere, somehow. And that'll be something else we've checked on the list – we'll have spent a whole night together. I know it's maybe not the happy ending you were hoping for, but you probably weren't hoping for a happy ending anyway, because you already know about the Time of the Static. Unless you're reading this in the next six weeks, and I'm sure as hell not going to show anybody. How is it where you are? Have people learned their lesson? How was that show about the three-inch rock star? Maybe they canceled it.

Not a Star

I found out that my son was the star of a porn film when Karen Glenister from two doors down dropped an envelope through our letter-box. Inside the envelope was a video and a little note which said:

Dear Lynn,

I'm not in the habit of dropping smutty films through people's letter-boxes! But I thought you and Frank might be interested in this one! It's not mine, I should add! Carl was at a mate's house on Friday night after they'd been out drinking, and his mate put this tape on, you know what they're like! And Carl recognized Someone You Might Know. He couldn't stop laughing. I had no idea! Does he get this from his Dad?!? You've kept it quiet if he does!!!!

Love

Karen

It had to be her, didn't it? It had to be Karen bloody Glenister. She's a nurse at the hospital, so she knows everyone and everything. And whatever she finds out, she passes on to whoever happens to be standing around, whether it's their business or not, and whether they're interested or not. She knew Dave had had the snip about ten minutes before I did, and half the town knew about it five minutes later. Everything has to go through her. She's the Clapham Junction of gossip. So it would be her son that saw Mark's film; it couldn't not have been. It's the law around here.

I was the only one in when I picked the envelope up off of the doormat. Dave wasn't back from work, and Mark plays five-a-side after college on Wednesdays. I opened the envelope at the kitchen table, read the note, and then looked at the video, which was called . . . Listen, if I'm going to tell this story, I'll have to use some words that might offend you. But if I don't say them, you won't get any sense of the shock I felt. So. The film was called *Meet the Fuckers*, and there was a picture of Mark on the cover. He was standing behind a woman with enormous boobs, and he had his hands over them so that you couldn't see her nipples.

My knees started to shake. I couldn't stand up, and I could hardly breathe. I hadn't seen the film then, so I still had the luxury of imagining that my son didn't really *do* very much, apart from stand behind topless women and cover their nipples with his hands. I think there might even have been a brief moment when I told myself Mark was just being a gentleman – that there was this poor girl, caught with no blouse, thankful that Mark was there to hide her shame . . . You know what it's like when you've got kids. You'll only believe the worst of them when you've got no other choice.

I found it impossible to get my head around. Mark! I thought. My Mark! Mark, who used to sit at the kitchen table trying to do his English homework, and finding it so difficult that he chewed his way right through his biro,

night after night! At first, I didn't know why that partic-
ular memory made the video seem so hard to believe.
There must have been millions of people who took their
clothes off for a living, and every single one of them
probably found their English homework a bit of a strug-
gle. Or is that just me being prejudiced? Could you come
top in English and then go on to star in a film called
Meet the Fuckers? It's hard to imagine, isn't it?.

But then I worked out why the biro-chewing didn't
seem to fit with the career in porn. Mark is . . . Well,
he's never been the star of anything. He's been trying
to get a leisure and tourism qualification so as he can
get a job in a sports centre somewhere, but he's finding
the studying hard. We're worried it might be too much
for him, that he's set his sights too high. Anyway, when
I saw him on the cover of that video, I realized that
we'd got used to the idea of thinking of him as, I don't
know. *Not special.* I mean, he's special because he's our
son. But it seemed to me that the two words I'd said to
him most over the last few years were 'Never mind'.
School reports, exam results, job applications, football
trials, girlfriends: 'Never mind', 'Never mind', 'Never
mind'. I haven't really seen any porn films – only what
was on the TV when we were on holiday in Spain, when
we found that German cable channel. But if someone
had told me that Mark had appeared in one and asked
me to guess what sort of part he played, I'd have said
he was the husband who discovered his wife in bed with
the window-cleaner or something like that. I'd never
have guessed that he'd be on the cover. Sad, isn't it, the
way you sort of give up on your kids?

So it was like I had to get used to this whole new life – a life in which Mark had something that marked him out, made him different to everyone else. I had no idea what that something was, though. That was the next big shock.

I know this sounds funny, but I probably hadn't thought about Mark's penis since the day he was born. I mean, I didn't even think about it very much then, but that was the last time it actually sort of meant something to me. Because on the day he was born, his penis was who he was, if you know what I mean. The midwife held him up and said, 'It's a little boy,' and I looked, and it was. So Mark was Mark, and not Olivia, which was who he would have been if he didn't have one. And after that . . . Well, I washed him and everything, until he was old enough to do it himself, and then that was it. Our relationship was over. Even when he started seeing girls, and Dave and I were wondering whether he was sleeping with them, I never thought about that actual part of him. I told Dave to talk to him about contraception and the rest of it, and when I thought about his sex life . . . Well, I tried not to. Once, when he was seventeen or so, I walked into his bedroom on a Thursday afternoon, and he was in there with Lisa, his girlfriend at the time. They weren't naked or anything, but they weren't doing their homework either, and his hands were all over her. I just walked out again, and I got Dave to talk to him later, about what would happen if he got someone pregnant, what it would cost him. (I left Dave to work that bit out, because – never

mind, never mind – I couldn't.) But I never said anything.
I wished I hadn't seen what I saw, though. It was as if
I'd walked in on my mum and dad doing something. I
suppose someone's written a book about sex and the
family, because it's obviously an important and difficult
subject. But the trouble is, you wouldn't want to read
it, would you?

I had to think about all of it – Mark's penis and sex and
the family, everything – when I put the video on. I didn't
watch it all. I couldn't. (And it wasn't just because Mark
was in it, or because it was filthy. It was also rubbish,
cheap and vulgar and depressing, like a naked version
of an old 70s sitcom. The girl with the big breasts, for
example, was supposed to be French, so of course she
said 'Ooh la la!' It was about all she did say.) But I saw
enough to understand why Mark was on the cover. It
was the biggest one I've ever seen. OK, I haven't seen
many, but you see them around more than you used to,
don't you? You see them in films, and some of the girls
at work have posters and postcards up, and Dave isn't
the only man I've ever slept with. And I can honestly
say that the ones I've seen were all pretty much the
same size, give or take. Mark's, though . . . It looked
like it didn't belong to him. It looked like it was a special
effect. In fact, the only reason I knew for sure it was
real was because no one in their right minds would put
Mark in a film if it wasn't for his thing. He can't act to
save his life, and you could hardly hear what he says
because he mumbles so badly, and it's not even as if he
looks like Tom Cruise. He's nice-looking, I think, but

no one would go to the trouble of making an enormous penis for him. Mark was special, after all. We'd
never have to say 'Never mind' about that.

You're probably thinking to yourself, 'Hold on. She
really had no idea? Is she blind or stupid?' And as the
film was going on, and I watched these girls rolling their
eyes in disbelief (that wasn't all they did, but there was
a lot of eye-rolling, and I was grateful for it), I tried to
work out whether I'd missed any clues the last few years.

And the first thing I remembered is that he didn't like
taking communal showers – there had been a thing
about it at school, and in the end we'd had to write a
note to his games teacher. Neither of us ever sat him
down to ask him what the problem was; he'd just told
us that he didn't like them, felt funny about them. Dave
was even worried that he might be queer, but we'd
already found a couple of girly magazines under his
bed, so that theory didn't make much sense. And then
I started to think about his thing with trousers. He's
always preferred baggy ones – he hasn't ever worn jeans
or anything like that, and we've always teased him a bit
because he's ended up looking so straight. He's got more
suits than any normal twenty-three-year-old – he buys
them in the Oxfam shop and places like that – and he's
got endless pairs of what my mum would have called
'slacks', trousers with creases in them made out of
flannel or whatever. He always said that other kids were
all scruffy and dirty, and that no one knew how to dress
properly any more, but now I could see that he'd
invented his look to get himself out of a tight spot, as
it were. His clothes never seemed to fit with the rest of

his personality, or the music he liked, or the friends he knocked around with, so we could never really understand it, but that was because we didn't have all the information we needed. Oh, plus: he stopped me buying his pants. He was clever about it, because he said I didn't understand about things like that, pants and socks and vests, but, looking back, I can see it was the pants part of it all that he was worried about. He didn't like slips much, and he didn't like boxers; he'd only wear something he calls boxer briefs, which are sort of like trunks, but with a pouch to put it in. They look a bit show-offy, the sort of thing a male stripper might wear, and Dave went back to thinking he was gay for a little while. But Mark had moved away from girly mags and on to real girls by this time, and it seemed to me that Mark was going to an awful lot of trouble just to prove he was straight if he wasn't. We didn't waste a lot of time puzzling it all out. He just had his quirks, that was all. Who doesn't?

I turned the video off and sat there for a moment. Dave was due back any minute, and Mark after he'd had a drink with his five-a-side team, and I didn't know what I was going to say to either of them. Maybe I didn't have to say anything. Maybe I could just march up to bloody Karen bloody Glenister's house, give her the film back and tell her that if she ever breathed a word to anybody about Mark's wotsit, I'd bash her over the head with it. But in my heart of hearts I knew it was too late.

Dave came in to find me sitting on the sofa staring at a blank TV screen.

'You all right?' he said.

'I've just had a bit of a shock,' I told him.

'What's up?' He sat down with me and took my hand and looked at me. He was frightened, and just for a moment I could see that finding out your son had a huge penis wasn't the same as finding out you had cancer, so I tried to smile.

'Oh, it's nothing. Really. It's just . . .' I reached down to my feet and picked up the video case and gave it to him. He laughed.

'What?' I said.

'Who gave you that?'

'Karen Glenister.'

'I can see why. That's funny.'

'What's funny?'

'He looks just like him, doesn't he? Have you shown him?'

'Not yet. He's at football. Dave . . .' I took a deep breath. 'It *is* Mark.'

He looked at me, and then he looked at the video, and then he looked at me again.

'How d'you mean?'

I put my hands up, as if to say, I don't know an easier way of explaining it.

'Mark?'

'Yeah.'

'In this film?'

'Yeah.'

'Doing what?'

I put my hands up again, although this time I meant, Well, what do people normally do in porn films?

'Why?'

'You'd have to ask him.'

'But, I mean . . . Why would they choose Mark? He's not . . . He can't . . .'

'Dave,' I said. 'Our son has the biggest . . . *thing* I've ever seen.'

We had a talk then, about the pants and the showers and the rest of it, and it was like one of those conversations you see on *ER* or something like that. You know, How did we miss the signs? How could we be so blind? Except in *ER* they're usually talking about prostitution or heroin addiction, which is a much more important thing, and the signs they're talking about aren't anywhere near as obvious. They have more of an excuse for their blindness.

'He's been hiding it,' said Dave, and that was the first time I actually laughed. 'He has, though, hasn't he? For years and years. Bloody hell.'

'What did you want him to do?'

'I don't know. He could have talked to us.'

'Could he? He couldn't have talked to me.'

'Why not?'

'I'm his mother. He isn't going to tell me stuff like that. I wouldn't have let him, to be honest.'

'So it was my job?'

'It was nobody's job. What could you have done? Ask him every few months how it's coming along? It was up to him, Dave, and he didn't want to, you know. Share the load.'

The trouble is, you can't help it. Everything you say

sounds dirty, without you wanting it to, so you end up cracking jokes about your own son's private parts. It seemed unhealthy but unavoidable, like breathing bad air when you live beside a motorway.

'You going to watch the film?' I asked Dave.

'No. No way. I can't watch that.' The way he said it, with the emphasis on the 'I', irritated me, as if he was superior in some way.

'Yeah, well it wasn't as if I wanted to.'

'You did, though, didn't you? Even after you'd seen his picture on the cover. You knew what you'd see.'

'I really didn't.'

'I'm sorry,' he said after a while. 'It's just, you know . . . It just seemed like such a normal day. I didn't think I'd come home to find my whole life had changed.'

I didn't say anything. But I could have pointed out that most life-changing days happen without you expecting them. I've spent what seems like half my life expecting the worst, and it never happens. But on the day it does, it'll knock me flat on my back anyway.

Mark came in about eleven. We're usually upstairs getting ready for bed by then, but we'd waited up, for obvious reasons, and he was surprised to see us there, sat on the sofa watching TV.

'Is there something good on?'

Dave didn't even turn round to look at him.

'No. Not really,' I said. 'We just started watching this film, and now we want to see how it finishes.'

'I'm going to make myself a sandwich.'

'OK, son.'

He always comes in from the pub and makes himself a sandwich on football nights, which is why Dave had left the video on the kitchen table. That way, he'd know we'd cottoned on to him without us having to say anything. We didn't really have a plan after that. I suppose we thought there'd be an argument, and then eventually a chat; but the next thing we heard was the front door slamming.

'Shit,' said Dave. 'Now what?'

'Where's he gone, d'you think?'

'I don't know, do I?'

'Supposing he's left home?'

'People don't leave home like that. People don't say, "I'm going to make myself a sandwich," and then, bang, they're gone.'

I didn't say anything, but from what I could tell, that was exactly what people did. You can watch the local news just about any night of the week and see some mother talking about how her son never even said good-bye. And then there's a phone number appealing for information.

'He might have gone round Becca's, I suppose,' said Dave.

'Shall I call her?'

'No. Give him some time. If we don't hear from him tomorrow, we'll call then.'

Becca was Mark's girlfriend. She had her own place a few streets away, but Mark didn't usually stay there during the week, because Becca had a flatmate with a boyfriend up North. He usually spends the weekends round there, when they've got the place to themselves.

I hadn't thought about Becca up until now, but once Dave had mentioned her, I couldn't help it. What . . . ? How . . . ? I had to stop myself, but Dave and I both went quiet at the same time, so I'm sure we were thinking about the same thing.

Just then, we heard the key in the lock, and Mark came in and sat down in the armchair. For a moment all three of us watched the TV.

'I thought there was something wrong when you said you wanted to see how the film turned out,' Mark said, and it was only then I realized that we were watching Man United beating a French team.

'How did you find it?'

'Karen Glenister put it through the letter-box.'

'Karen Glenister? What was she doing with it?'

'Carl saw it round a mate's house, and borrowed it when he recognized you.'

'Have you watched it?'

'I have. Your dad hasn't.'

'And I won't,' Dave said, as if Mark was trying to persuade him.

'How do other people cope?' I said.

'Which other people?' Mark asked.

'Other mothers. Families. I mean, they all have mothers, don't they, porn stars?'

'I'm not a porn star,' said Mark.

'What are you, then?' said Dave.

'I'm not a star, am I? Stars are people like Jenna Jameson and Ron Jeremy.'

'Who?'

'They're porn stars. You wouldn't know them.'

'Exactly. So you could be a porn star, for all I know. You might be the most famous porn star in Britain, and I wouldn't have a clue.'

'You think Ron Jeremy lives at home with his mum and dad?'

'He might do! I don't know who Ron Jeremy is! "Ron Jeremy." He sounds like exactly the sort of person who lives with his mum and dad.'

I was getting frustrated. I didn't want to talk about where Ron Jeremy lived. I wanted to talk to my son about what he was doing with his life.

'How did this start?' said Dave. 'How long has it been going on? How many films are there?'

For some reason, it hadn't occurred to me for a moment that there'd be others.

'It started . . . Well. Sort of through Becca.'

'Becca? She's a porn star too?'

Mark sighed. 'Mum. Becca works in a playgroup. You know that.'

'I don't know anything any more. I don't know what she does.'

'So when we went to their Christmas play last year, you thought that was a set-up, or what? Becca doesn't know anything about . . . you know. My other job.'

'But you just said . . .'

'Will you let me talk? You know Becca's got a flatmate? And this flatmate's got a boyfriend who lives in Manchester? Well, that's what he does. He makes porn films.'

'Oh, well,' said Dave. 'That explains everything. You couldn't really help it, could you? If your girlfriend's flatmate's boyfriend makes porn films in Manchester, you pretty much had to help him out. I mean, once you've had a call from him . . . Must be like getting a phone call from the Queen. You can't say no. And how come Becca doesn't know anything about it?'

'Because . . . You really want to go into this?'

'Yes. We both do,' said Dave.

'It means talking about some pretty embarrassing stuff.'

'I don't want to talk about what you do. Just how you got involved. How it happened.'

'It still means saying things you might not want to talk about.'

'We know everything,' said Dave. 'Your mum's seen the film, remember.'

'Yeah, well. Seeing isn't the same as talking. We could just leave it at that, and never mention it again.'

'How could we not mention it again?' I said. 'How could we sit here night after night eating our tea, with all that going on?'

'Not much goes on, most of the time,' said Mark. 'Most of the time, I'm not making porn films.'

'How did it happen?' said Dave.

'You've seen the film, Mum,' said Mark. 'So you know . . .' He stopped. 'Oh, bloody hell. I can't talk about this to you two. I've spent the last whatever it is, ten years, not talking to you about this.'

'I've seen it,' I said. 'I've seen the film, and I've seen . . . I've seen why they'd want you in it.'

'OK,' said Mark. 'Right. Good.'

He stopped again. We've never had problems talking, in our family. Usually everyone's talking at once, so these pauses and silences were something new for us. Obviously we've been talking about the wrong things all these years. It's easy to talk about nothing much.

'Becca,' said Dave, as if Mark had lost his thread.

'Becca,' said Mark. 'When we first started going out, she had a chat with Rache. Her flatmate.'

'What sort of chat?'

'A whatever. A girly chat, sort of thing. About me. And my problem. Which had sort of become her problem too, if you catch my drift.'

'Oh.'

'And Rache passed the information on. To her boyfriend. And he phoned me. And we went on from there. And Becca never knew nothing about it.'

'You've never told her?'

'Course not. You know Becca, Mum. She wouldn't understand.'

'And what happens if she finds out?'

'I'll be looking for a new girlfriend, I should think.'

He liked Becca, but I knew he wasn't going to end up with her, and so did he. They were already at that point where it was so comfortable that Mark was becoming uncomfortable, and there was definitely an element of Russian roulette in this. If the decision to split were taken out of his hands, he'd have been grateful.

'Hold on, hold on. Rewind,' said Dave. 'You went on from there.'

'Yeah.'

'But *why* did you go on from there?'

'Why?' Mark repeated the question as if Dave were weird for asking it.

'Yeah. Why?'

Mark shrugged. 'A bit of extra cash, obviously . . . And I was interested. Plus, I dunno. This probably sounds mad, but, I mean . . . I haven't really got another, like, talent, have I? I watch all these people, like Beckham and all them. And they're entitled to make money out of what they're born with. Up until I met Robbie, Rache's boyfriend, it had never done anything for me. And I thought, What's the difference? What's the difference between, I don't know, having a . . . Having what I've got and, and being able to play the piano?'

'What's the difference?' said Dave. 'You can't see what the difference is?'

'No,' said Mark. 'Tell me.'

'Having a big thing isn't a talent, is it? Playing the piano is hard. I mean, what you've got doesn't . . . you know. It's not *hard*. It doesn't give people *pleasure*.'

Mark and I stared at the carpet. I was trying not to laugh. Everything sounded like a Benny Hill joke. Eventually Dave caught on, and it didn't make anything better. It could have been one of those moments that you see on TV, when everyone starts to laugh together, and the problem no longer seems as big as it did. But Dave just lost his rag.

'It's not fucking funny.'

'No one's laughing,' I said.

'You were trying not to.'

'I don't know what more we can do than not laugh at something you don't think is funny.'

'But you still saw the joke. I can't see the joke. My son is a porn star. Where's the joke in that?'

'I'm not a porn . . .'

'Whatever. You're a freak, Mark. Being a freak isn't the same thing as having a talent.'

Dave was angry, but there's still no excuse, is there? You can't call your own kid a freak and expect him to take it on the chin.

'You know it's wotsit, don't you?' said Mark. 'Hereditary?'

He knew what he was doing. He must have guessed years ago that he and Dave didn't share the same problem, otherwise it would have come up by now. (Oh, for God's sake . . .) People say that when men argue, what they're arguing about, underneath it all is, Who's got the biggest? And here were my two men, my husband and my son, arguing about exactly that – except there was no argument. I'm probably the only person in the world who's seen both of them, and there was no need for a tape measure, if you know what I mean. Mark won, hands down. (Is that dirty, 'Hands down'? It sounds dirty, doesn't it? But I don't know what it would mean.)

'Yeah? Well, you don't get it from me. Mine's normal. Isn't it, Lynn?'

'Normal? Is that what you call it?'

It was just a little joke, an attempt to jolly everyone along. On a normal evening, no one would have taken offence, but this wasn't a normal evening, and offence was taken. I wasn't even thinking about the size thing. I'd forgotten for a split second what wasn't normal, so I didn't mean to suggest that Dave's was small. (It's not.

It's . . . Well, it's normal.) I just meant that it wasn't, I don't know, curved, or covered in green and yellow spots, or it could talk. That sort of abnormal. Jokey abnormal, not opposite-of-Mark's abnormal. If I'd thought it through, I wouldn't have said anything; if I'd thought it through, I wouldn't have found myself lying in bed at one in the morning talking to Dave about an affair I had twenty-five years ago.

'You know that thing with Steve?'

'No.'

'Steve. Steve Laird. You know.'

'Oh. Yeah.'

It wasn't as though I was playing dumb, because I don't think I've heard his name since we got married. But even so, it wasn't like he appeared in the middle of our bed that night completely out of nowhere. I can't explain it, but when Dave brought Steve up, it sort of made sense. There was sex in the air that night, and it wasn't safe sex, if you know what I mean – it wasn't the comfortable, enjoyable sex that Dave and I have, the sort of sex you don't even have to think about. The sex we'd been breathing was a dark, scary sex, and it was as if Dave had converted it into the only thing he had to hand.

'Was that what it was about?' he asked me.

'What?'

'That.'

'What's that?'

'You know.'

'No.'

'That. Normal. Not normal.'

'Are you asking me whether your penis is too small? Or whether Steve had a bigger one than you?'

'Shut up.'

'OK. I will.'

I listened to him breathing in the dark, and I knew we weren't finished. It wasn't much of an affair, really. I wasn't married, for a start, although Dave and I were living together, and we were unofficially engaged. I only slept with Steve two or three times, and the sex wasn't anything much. It certainly wasn't the point, although what the point was I don't exactly remember now. Something to do with feeling I was in a rut? And I know that Dave was in two minds about everything, and he had a flirtation going with this girl at work which he said never went anywhere, although I was never quite sure . . .

'Yeah,' he said, like about five minutes later.

'Yeah what?'

'Yeah, that's what I'm asking.'

'Of course it wasn't about that. You know it wasn't.'

'Right.'

'And I can't answer the other question. Not because the answer would upset you, but because I can't remember. You know it doesn't matter, don't you?'

'Yeah. Well, I know that's what you're supposed to say, anyway.'

'It's the truth. It's like, I don't know. It wouldn't have mattered if he was taller than you or not.'

'It would have mattered if I'd been five foot and he'd been six foot.'

'Yeah. But. Five foot is pretty small. You're not small like that, are you?'

'Oh, so what am I small like?'

'You're not small. For Christ's sake, Dave. You're smaller than your son. But I've seen your son, and believe me, you wouldn't want to be like him. Neither would I want you to be like him. Oh, and Steve wasn't like him, either.'

'You just said you couldn't remember.'

'You think I wouldn't remember something like that? Blimey. If he'd been like Mark, I'd have had to talk to one of those therapists people see after disasters.'

'I'm sorry,' said Dave. I love Dave for loads of reasons, and one of them is that he always knows when he's making a berk of himself. 'It's been a weird evening, though, hasn't it?'

I laughed. 'You could say that, yes.'

'What are we going to do?'

'I'm not sure we can do anything. It's his life. There are worse things to worry about.'

'Are there?'

'Yeah. Course. Drugs. Violence. All that stuff.'

'Porn's like drugs, though, isn't it? I mean, they're both a menace to society,' Dave said.

'Put it this way. All those nights we've lain here listening for him to come home late at night . . . You worry about whether he's been stabbed, or whether he's been taking crack, or whether he's driving home pissed. But have you ever stayed awake worrying he's been making a porno film?'

'No. But that's because I never thought of it before.'

'Yeah, and why didn't you think of it?'

'I dunno. I never thought he had it in him.'

'That's not it. You never thought of it because it couldn't kill him. If it could have killed him, I would've thought about it, because I've thought about everything else.'

'What about AIDS?'

I got up, put my dressing gown on and hammered on Mark's door.

'What?'

'What about AIDS?'

'Go to bed.'

'No. Not until you've talked to me.'

'I'm not going into any details. But I'm not daft.'

'You'd better give me a few more details than that. That's not good enough.'

'Thanks a bunch. There is absolutely nothing whatsoever to worry about.'

'I just want to say one more thing,' said Dave when I'd gone back to bed.

'Go on.'

'One more thing about Mark's, you know. His talent.'

'If you must.'

'If it's hereditary . . . It must have been your dad.'

My dad . . . Jesus.

I hope this never happens to you, but when you get your dad's thing and your son's thing dangled in your face, all on the same day . . . Well, you can imagine. It's not the sort of day you never want to end.

I went to sleep all right, though, because for some

reason that I can't and don't really want to explain, Dave and I ended up having sex that night, and it wasn't the sort of sex we usually have. It was more his idea than mine, but, you know. I joined in.

My mum lives with my sister Helen in Walthamstow, a couple of miles away. It's just one of those things that happened: Helen got divorced soon after Dad died, and she's never had kids, and it just seemed like a happy solution for everyone – especially, if I'm honest, for me and Dave. Helen moans about it a bit to me, tries to make me feel guilty and so on, but the arrangement suits her, really. It's not like Mum's a geriatric. She's only sixty-eight, and she's pretty fit, and she goes out a lot – she goes out more than Helen, in fact. Helen says that Mum stops her from meeting anybody, but the only way that would work is if Mum's actually copping off with the men that Helen is interested in.

I went round to see them on the Saturday morning. I bumped into Karen Glenister on the way to the bus stop; she just happened to be putting her recycling out the very moment I walked past her front door, and if you believe that you'll believe anything.

'So,' she said.

'Hello, Karen.' I gave her a big smile.

'Did you watch it?'

'Oh, I've seen it all before,' I said. 'Did Carl enjoy it?'

She looked at me. 'He wasn't looking at Mark, you know.'

'Oh, course not. I'm sure he'll get a girlfriend soon enough.'

'And does he get it off his dad?'

'Have you ever wondered why I'm always so cheerful?' I said. And then I just kept walking.

I hadn't made up my mind whether I was going to try and talk to Mum. We've never had that kind of conversation before, and once you get to a certain age, you're tempted to think that you've got away with it, aren't you? But it just seemed important. When Dad died, I went through that business of regretting that I hadn't spent enough time talking to him; I loved him, but I seemed to spend a lot of time resenting him, and trying to avoid him, and getting pissed off with him. And now I was trying to work out whether this business was something I should know. Was it a part of him? And if so, was it a good part or a bad part?

Dad was really sick for the last couple of years of his life, and sick is how I remembered him best. But when I found out about this other thing, I started to think about him in a different way. I don't mean I started to think about him in, you know, a weird way. It's just that knowing what I knew meant that I thought about him being healthy and young, or younger, anyway. It just seemed to follow. Because finding out something like that . . . You can't help but wonder about a period in his life when he would have been using it, if you know what I mean, and he couldn't have been using it much at the end, poor sod. And it really helped me to think about him in these other ways. I started to remember other things: the way he dressed when Helen and I were kids, for example – in trousers like Mark's, even though he must have been young in the sixties and seventies, when people were wearing tighter trousers. And on the bus that morning, I suddenly had a flash of the way he looked at my mum sometimes, and the way she looked at him. I'll tell you the truth: I suddenly got all weepy, on the top of the bus. I was sad, but it wasn't just sadness. There was something else in there, too – it was that happy/sad, sweet-and-sour feeling you can get when you look at baby photos of your grown-up kids. I don't know. When you get older, it feels like happy memories and sad memories come to pretty much the same thing. It's all just emotion, in the end, and any of it can make you weep. Anyway, when I'd dabbed at my eyes a bit, I almost started to laugh. Because who'd have thought that what began with Karen Glenister dropping a porn film through the letter-box would end up with that sort of stuff going through your head?

Mum wasn't in, but Helen was.

'When will she be back?'

'She's only gone down to get her fags,' said Helen. 'I've stopped her smoking in here, did I tell you? She has to go outside.'

'You'll kill her,' I said. It was only a joke, but you can't really joke with Helen.

'Oh, right. I'll kill her, not the fags.'

'Yeah. Ironic, eh?'

She made me a cup of coffee and we sat down at the kitchen table.

'So what's new? I could do with some gossip.'

I laughed. I couldn't help it.

'What?'

'I don't know. Gossip.'

'What about it?'

'People never really have any, do they? People always say, "Got any gossip?" but if they have to ask, it means there isn't any. Because if there is any, they come out with it straight away.'

I didn't know where I was going with this, or how much I wanted to say.

'So what you're saying is you've got nothing to tell me.'

'Not really.'

And that was the moment I decided to tell her – just when I'd told her that I had nothing to tell her. It just seemed like too good an opportunity to miss. I get on OK with Helen, but she can be really prissy, and I suddenly saw that she'd find out anyway, sooner or later, and that I'd always regret not telling her myself, because I could choose the best moment. And the best moment was the moment she was least expecting it: I wanted the look on her face to be something I'd remember for ever, something I'd be describing to Dave, and maybe even to Mark, over and over again.

'One funny thing, I suppose,' I said. 'Karen Glenister dropped this porn film through the door, and you'll never guess who's in it?'

She was already making this fantastic face, like she was being throttled by an invisible hand – she was going all pop-eyed and purple. I could have left it at that and she'd have needed to take deep breaths for the rest of the day.

'Do you want to know?' I said after a while, when she still hadn't said anything.

'Go on,' she said.

'Mark,' I said. 'Our Mark. Your nephew.'

'What do you mean, "In a porn film"?'

'What do you think I mean? What else could I mean, other than what I've just said? When people say that Hugh Grant's in *Love Actually*, what do they mean?'

'*Love Actually* isn't a porn film, though, is it?'

'What difference does that make?'

'I dunno. When you say that a famous actor is in a film, you're not saying very much, are you? I mean, there's nothing that's difficult to understand. But when you tell me that my nephew's in a porn film . . . I thought for a moment there was something I'm not getting. That you were using some slang I'd never heard before.'

I wanted to laugh at her, but I couldn't laugh at that, because I knew what she meant. It was sort of what I felt when I saw the cover of the video: that there was something about the photo that wasn't in my language, or wasn't aimed at my age group. I feel that way sometimes when Mark's watching that comedy programme when some man dressed as a woman says 'Yeah, but, no, but . . .' and he just starts laughing.

Now I think about it, this whole thing with Mark is like an episode of *Little Britain*, because I don't know whether it's funny or not.

'No,' I said. 'That's what I'm saying. Mark's in a porn film, like Hugh Grant was in *Love Actually*. It turns out he's got an enormous penis, and, and . . .'

Helen was staring at me, trying hard to listen, trying hard to understand.

'I suppose he didn't know what to do with it,' she said. 'I suppose there *isn't* much you can do with it, if you think about it.'

'You could just leave it in your trousers,' I said.

'Well, yes. There's that.'

'You weren't going to tell Mum, were you?'

'I don't know. I don't know why I came, really. Except the penis thing is supposed to be hereditary, and Dave hasn't got it. I mean, he's just got a normal one.'

'Well, Mum hasn't . . . Oh, my God! You mean Dad?'

'Yes.'

'But he didn't . . . He couldn't have had.'

'Why not? I don't know. Do you?'

'No. God. Of course I don't. No. God. You just going to come out and ask her?'

'I don't know. I'll see what I feel like when she gets back.'

Mum came in, sat down, took the cellophane off her cigarettes, then with a sigh and a little mutter, she remembered that she had to go outside.

'I'll come out with you,' I said.

'You can have one here,' said Helen.

'Why?'

'Lynn doesn't come over that often. I don't want to have to look at her through the window.'

But she was worried she was going to miss something, you could tell. She got a saucer off the draining board and put it down on the table, for the ash.

'Did Dad ever smoke?' I asked Mum. It was a start. Maybe he always liked a post-coital fag, and it would be a short step from talking about that to asking her whether . . .

'No,' she said.

'Never?'

'I don't know about never. But he never smoked when he was with me. And he hated me smoking. Always on at me to give up. I wish I had. For him, I mean. He never asked for much, and I wouldn't even give him that.'

She stubbed her cigarette out in disgust, half-smoked, as if she were giving up now, four years too late.

'He only nagged because he was worried about you,' I said. 'As it happens, there was nothing to worry about. You're still with us, and you're still fagging away.'

But there was no joking her out of it – her eyes were glistening, and all we could do now was drag her back and away from that horrible, dark, deep pit that she fell into after Dad died. Who was I to push her back into it? I changed the subject, and we ended up talking about things that none of us could get upset about: why Mum won't use the halal butcher, whether *Big Brother* is fake (Helen's got a thing about that), and the family, including Mark. I told Mum he was ticking along, and Helen caught my eye, and I thought she was going to giggle. But there's no joke in 'ticking along', is there? Where's the pun in that?

Mark had a baby brother, for about two hours on the morning of June the fifth, 1984. We called him Nicky, and he was born with a heart defect, and he died in an incubator, without ever quite being alive. I'm over it now, of course I am; I was over it within a year or two. But I thought of the baby when I saw my mum struggling with the memory of my dad – not just because of the grief, but because I could see how lucky I was. I'm forty-nine years old, and those two deaths, Nicky and my dad, were the worst days of my life; nothing else has even come close. What else would there be? Dave had a car accident and broke his arm, Mark got pneumonia when he was little, but they were frightening for a moment or two, not devastating. And Mark's film career didn't even matter as much as either of the frightening things. I've been disappointed, loads and loads of times – who hasn't? – but I wasn't even entirely sure that Mark's new career was disappointing. Like I said, it might even have been funny, and something that has the potential to be funny . . . Well, that's a whole different category. If you think that something might be funny, looked at in the right way, then look at it in the right way.

On the bus going home, I thought about what had happened since I found out that Mark was in a porn video, and what I realized was, all of it was good. The conversation I had with Dave about Steve Laird was tricky, for a while, but then we ended up having great sex. I really enjoyed being cheeky to Karen Glenister, and on the bus going down to Mum's I'd had that little blub, and even that was because of being able to swap some miserable memories for some happy ones. Throw in a nice cup of coffee with Mum and Helen (which would never have happened if I hadn't decided, for reasons best known to myself, to try and find out how big my father's thing was) and I can honestly say that it's an experience I could recommend to anyone. Can that be right?

Mark was making himself some lunch when I got back – he was frying up what looked like half a pound of bacon.

'Blimey,' I said. 'Someone's starving.'

He looked at me.

'Yeah. I am. But not because I've been doing anything, if that's what you mean.'

'That's not what I meant. Calm down. Not everything I say is going to be about that.'

'Sorry.'

I watched him make a mess of turning the bacon over, and took the wooden spatula thing off him.

'Do bad things happen to the girls in those films?'

'How do you mean?'

'Are they, I dunno, all on drugs, or on the game or something?'

'No. That one I was . . . The one you saw, Vicky, she's a travel agent. She just got fed up with her breasts the way I got fed up with . . . me. There's a few that want to do topless modelling, but that's about it. Rachel's boyfriend, he loves making films. He wants to be Steven Spielberg, and this is as close as he can get for the moment.'

'He's rubbish,' I said. 'They make *Carry On* look like *Dances with Wolves* or something.'

'He's terrible,' said Mark. 'I don't want to stop, Mum.'

'Oh. Why not?'

'It doesn't make any difference, you and Dad finding out. I wasn't doing it because I could get away with it, you know.'

'So how long do you want to do it for?'

'I dunno. 'Til I'm on my feet, I suppose.'

'Make me a promise.'

I didn't know until I said it what I wanted from him, but when I came out with it, it sounded right.

'Stop when something worse happens.'

'What does that mean?'

'You know. When, I don't know . . . When your Gran dies. Or when your dad and I get divorced or something. Stop then.'

'Why d'you say that?'

'I don't know. It just felt right.'

'But shouldn't it be the other way round? I mean . . . When something bad happens, you won't notice this.'

'No. But I'll know it's there, that's the thing. I don't want to know it's there when I don't feel the same as I do now.'

'How do you feel now?'

'I feel OK. That's the thing.'

He shrugged. 'All right, then. I promise. Unless you know for a fact you're getting divorced in the next week or so.'

'No, we're all right for the time being.'

He reached out his hand and we shook. 'Deal,' he said, and we left it at that.

*

That night, the three of us went out to the Crown for a drink before our dinner. We used to do it quite a lot when Mark was in his late teens, and it was a novelty for us all, but then Mark found better things to do, and we stopped. It wasn't like this huge thing, all deciding that we should spend quality time together in order to get to know each other better; it just happened. Dave said he fancied going out for a drink, and Mark and I were in the same sort of mood. But I was glad that somehow the film had moved us back in time, rather than forward – that we'd somehow ended up doing something we used to do. It needn't have been that way.

Anyway, I had this strange moment. Admittedly I'd been drinking lager on an empty stomach, but when Dave was getting the drinks in, and Mark was playing on the fruit machine, it was as if I floated out of myself and saw the three of us, all in our different places, all apparently cheerful, and I thought, I'd have settled for this on just about any day of my life since Nicky died. I wouldn't have settled for it before I got married, but you don't know, then, do you? You don't know how scared you'll feel, how many compromises you're prepared to make; you don't know that just about anything which looks OK on the outside can be made to feel OK on the inside. You don't know it has to work that way round.

POCKET PENGUINS